Benjy
and the Power of
Zingies

Weekly Reader Books presents

BENJY
and the Power of
ZINGIES

Jean Van Leeuwen

pictures by *Margot Apple*

THE DIAL PRESS · NEW YORK

This book is a presentation of
Weekly Reader Books.
Weekly Reader Books offers book clubs for children
from preschool through junior high school.

For further information write to:
Weekly Reader Books
1250 Fairwood Ave.
Columbus, Ohio 43216

Published by
The Dial Press
1 Dag Hammarskjold Plaza
New York, New York 10017

Library of Congress Cataloging in Publication Data
Van Leeuwen, Jean. Benjy and the power of Zingies.
Summary: Third-grader Benjy, tired of being small for
his age, decides to build up his body by eating the
breakfast cereal of sports stars.
[1. Food habits—Fiction. 2. Size and shape—Fiction.
3. Physical fitness—Fiction] I. Title.
PZ7.V3273Be [Fic] 82–1513
ISBN 0–8037–0379–1 AACR2
ISBN 0–8037–0380–5 (lib. bdg.)

To David, my Superstar

J.V.L.

1

Benjy was wearing his shirt with the number forty-two on it. He had on his best kicking sneakers. And he had eaten a big bowl of Zingies for breakfast. Zingies, the breakfast cereal of sports stars. The breakfast cereal even of Clyde Johnson, the greatest baseball player in the world. So he would have to do well in kickball today.

"Come on, Benjy," called Jason, hopping up and down on second base. "Slam one."

"Yeah, slam one right to me," yelled Alex. "If you can kick that far."

That Alex. He thought he was so great just because he was as big as a fourth-grader. Big deal. He was as big as a fourth-grader because he was supposed to be in fourth grade. Benjy would show him. The Armstrong team would cream the Bloom team today.

Alex rolled the ball. Benjy got his foot back. He kicked with all his power.

The ball blooped up in the air.

"Easy out!" yelled Alex. "I got it."

Benjy ran anyway. Maybe Alex would drop the ball. Anyway, he liked to run. When he ran, he pretended he was Marty Fox, stealer of the most bases in the American League. Marty Fox was a little guy like Benjy, but he was dangerous.

Benjy rounded first base and looked over. The ball was coming down right into Alex's arms. He didn't even have to move to catch it. And he didn't drop it either. Alex never dropped the ball.

"You're out. Too bad, Shrimpo." Alex grinned to show it really wasn't too bad. "We're up."

Benjy walked slowly out to the outfield. A pop fly. Why did he always have to kick pop flies? He did a few practice kicks in the air. Maybe it was his sneakers. Benjy looked down at them. It seemed like the rubber on the right toe was a little worn. He bet if his mother would buy him new ones—the blue kind with the white stripes on the side that looked like lightning—he'd be able to kick better. That was probably what he needed, new sneakers.

Brian was up now for the Bloom team. Alex's friend, Brian. He wasn't much bigger than Benjy, but he was a good kicker. Benjy moved in a little, close to third base. He squeezed his hands together. If Brian kicked a pop fly, he was going to catch it, and this time he wouldn't drop it. His hands would be like glue.

Spencer pitched. Brian kicked a good one, low and hard, right between Benjy and Danny, who was playing second base. Benjy raced after it. If he could get to the ball before it rolled down the hill, it might not be a home run.

But just as Benjy almost caught up to it, the ball hit a rock and took a crazy bounce. Off to the left and down the hill to the lower field. Right into the hands of the big kids.

"Oh, no," groaned Benjy.

Sometimes the big kids wouldn't give the ball back.

"Hey, give me the ball!" yelled Benjy.

"Why should I?" the kid who had it yelled back. He threw it to another kid, and the two of them ran off with the third-grade ball.

"Looks like the end of the game," said Danny.

"Yeah," said Benjy, digging his toe into the dirt. The worn-out toe. If he wore it out some more, his mother would have to buy him new sneakers. "Dumb fourth-graders."

It looked like a bad day.

And it didn't get better. At lunchtime Benjy found that his mother had given him sliced egg on granola bread in his lunch box. Disgusting. He had told her and told her that he only liked peanut butter and strawberry jam on white, but she thought that was too dull. She liked to surprise him. Benjy didn't like to be surprised at lunch.

He sat at the table just looking at his sandwich.

"Aren't you going to eat that?" asked Matthew hopefully. Matthew would eat anything. He looked it too. He was about as tall as two Benjys and as wide as three Benjys. About five Benjys altogether, Benjy figured. In his mind he called him Fat Matt.

"You can have it," Benjy told him.

"Really?" Matthew's face lit up like a Halloween pumpkin with a candle inside. "Thanks." He started stuffing the sandwich in without even checking to see what kind it was.

All Benjy had for lunch was milk and a banana.

His mother had even forgotten to put in a cookie. Some help she was.

After lunch was reading. That was bad too. He had to go to Miss Markoff, the special reading teacher. Benjy and Gretchen were the only ones who had to go. Gretchen the Pain, who sat next to Benjy and had funny hair and borrowed his pencils and gave them back with teeth marks on them. Everyone else in Mrs. Armstrong's class could read better than Benjy and Gretchen. They all got to read the blue book about Tim and his horse or the yellow one about fairy tales around the world. The book Benjy was reading was about Jack and his sister Sue and their dog Brownie. All Jack and Sue ever did was take Brownie for a walk in the park or visit their grandfather's farm or help their mother set the table. It was boring.

Benjy stared at the picture of Jack and Sue setting the table while Gretchen the Pain read out loud to Miss Markoff. He pretended that they did it all wrong and instead of smiling like she always did, their mother yelled at them and sent them to their rooms. But it was still boring. Mrs. Armstrong kept telling him that it would get better. She said that if he worked hard and had patience, soon he could read more interesting books. Books about wild animals and outer space and baseball. Maybe he could even read the book about Clyde Johnson, Superstar, in the library, the one with small print and hardly any pictures. But that seemed far away. Benjy didn't think he had that much patience.

They didn't even get to have second recess. It started to rain, and they had to stay in the gym and they couldn't even play ball because Gretchen the Pain and her friend Cynthia, the Kissing Machine, kept chasing all the boys, trying to kiss them.

And then on the way home on the bus Alex and Brian sat behind him. Benjy had thought he was lucky when they both got in the other third-grade class. But they still went on his bus. And that was unlucky. You couldn't tell what they would do. Once in the winter they had stuck a snowball down Benjy's jacket, and when he turned around, they were just looking out the window as if nothing had happened. Sometimes they grabbed his lunch box and emptied out all his stuff on the floor. He had to crawl around under the seats picking up his papers and colored pencils and fossilized rocks and baseball cards. One time they got hold of his entire feather collection and started blowing them all over the bus. He never did find his Canada goose feather again. Another time they had teased a kindergarten boy until he cried, and the bus driver had to stop the bus and make them sit up front. That was one thing though. They would never make Benjy cry.

"Hey, Shrimpo."

It was Alex. Benjy didn't turn around.

"Peewee."

He wouldn't look at them if they called him things like that. Just pretend they aren't there, he told himself.

"Benjy-baby."

Alex's face appeared around the side of the seat. "Hey, I'm talking to you."

If only Benjy had a boxing glove on, he'd let Alex have it, right in the nose. That would surprise him, all right. Instead, he mumbled, "What do you want?"

"Just wanted to tell you that you played a good game."

Benjy looked at him.

Alex's face was very serious. "Really," he said.

"Thanks," muttered Benjy.

"Yes, sir. Real good for a guy with a lead foot."

Alex's face disappeared, and there were whoops of laughter from the seat behind him.

"Very funny, you creeps," Benjy said. But he only said it loud enough for himself to hear.

It had been a bad day.

2

"Fifty-eight more days," sighed Benjy at breakfast the next morning.

"Fifty-eight more days until what?" asked his mother.

"Summer vacation," said Benjy.

His mother stopped feeding the baby her gloppy cereal.

"You're counting the days already?" she asked. "School must be getting you down."

"It's boring," said Benjy. "All we do is work. Reading, math, spelling, writing in script. Work, work, work."

"School is hard work," agreed his mother.

"And sometimes it rains at recess, so we can't go out. And the big kids take our kickball if it goes down to the lower field. And the boys' room is dirty," said Benjy.

"My," said Benjy's mother. "You do have problems. Is there anything about school that you like?"

Benjy thought about it. He watched his little sister blowing bubbles in her cereal, smiling from ear to ear. What did she know? Wait till she got to school.

"Art and recess," he said finally. "And once we saw a movie about snakes."

"I see," said his mother. "Well, I have to agree that it sounds kind of bleak. But maybe today will be better. Anyway, it's time for your bus."

Benjy packed up the things he was taking. His baseball cards, his colored pencils, a snap-together model of a brontosaurus that he'd painted himself, a piece of bone that might belong to some ancient animal, his postcard from the Museum of Natural History, and all his dinosaur books.

"That's a lot to carry," said his mother.

"I have to bring it," said Benjy. "We're starting to study dinosaurs today."

"Ah," said his mother. "Things may be looking up already."

Benjy started out the door. Then he came back. "Mom, can I get new sneakers after school today?" he asked. "These are all worn-out."

"Let me see your foot," said his mother.

Benjy lifted his right foot in the air.

"Absolutely not," said his mother.

She was right though. It was a better day. Mrs. Armstrong liked the books and the postcard and the brontosaurus model. She put the piece of bone on the display table and said they would try to find out what kind of animal it was. Then she talked about dinosaurs. She asked the class a lot of questions, and Benjy raised his hand for almost every one. That was because a long time ago, when he was about four, he had been crazy about dinosaurs. He used to go around with his pockets full of the little plastic ones from the five-and-ten, and even sleep with them under his pillow. His dinosaur books were worn-out from his mother and father reading them to him every night. Even though he wasn't crazy about dinosaurs anymore, he still remembered a lot of stuff about them.

And then Mrs. Armstrong said in her soft voice, "May seventeenth is Parents' Night. I was thinking that when your parents visit our room, it might be interesting for them to see what the world looked like in the Mesozoic Era. If each of you would like to choose a dinosaur to draw, we could make a mural for the back wall."

All of a sudden everyone was raising hands and talking at once.

"I want to make brontosaurus," said Matthew. He would. All brontosaurus ever did was stand around in lakes and eat up everything in sight.

"I'll do a flying reptile," said Gretchen the Pain.

"Can I make a volcano with flames shooting out?" asked Jason. He always liked to draw flames shooting out of things.

"Tyrannosaurus," said Benjy and Danny at the same time.

Mrs. Armstrong looked at both of them. Benjy held his breath. Tyrannosaurus was his favorite dinosaur. The biggest and meanest of all the meat-eaters.

"Let's let Benjy make tyrannosaurus," said Mrs. Armstrong, "since he brought in all this interesting reference material to share with us. Danny, you might like to do triceratops. It had three powerful horns on its head."

Benjy let out his breath slowly, making a little whistling sound. Things were definitely looking up.

He took out his colored pencils. Other kids got out crayons or markers. Mrs. Armstrong passed out the art paper. Everyone started to work. It was very quiet in the room.

Benjy thought he would copy the tyrannosaurus picture exactly the way it was in his favorite dinosaur book. He chose a dark green pencil. He started with the feet. Tyrannosaurus feet were hard to draw. There were three toes in front and one in back. You had to get each toe just right.

He had just finished the toes and was starting on the back legs when Mrs. Armstrong said, "It's time to put away your artwork and get ready for recess."

Benjy couldn't believe it. The morning was over already. He looked around. Some of the kids were finished with their pictures and were cutting them out. Jason was just putting the last touches on his flames, using red and yellow markers. "Watch out, they're hot," he was saying to Jennifer next to him. And Benjy had only done the toes.

He raised his hand.

"Is it all right to take my picture home and work on it?" he asked.

"Certainly, Benjy," said Mrs. Armstrong. She came over to look. "You've got a fine start on tyrannosaurus. Those are beautiful feet. Now, class, let's line up for recess."

Benjy got his jacket and got in line. He stood there, whistling under his breath.

"Want to play kickball?" asked Jason and Danny.

"Sure," said Benjy.

It had been a good morning. Better than good—terrific. They hadn't even had time to do any work.

3

When Benjy got home from school, his mother had the baby dressed in the fuzzy pink suit that made her look like a rabbit.

"Where are we going?" asked Benjy.

"You'll see," said his mother. She smiled mysteriously.

Benjy knew that smile. It meant his mother had one of her surprises up her sleeve. There was no use asking questions. Benjy got in the car.

They drove downtown. Maybe, thought Benjy, she had changed her mind and was going to buy him the sneakers that would make him a sports star after all. That would be a nice surprise.

But his mother drove right past the shoe store.

A haircut, thought Benjy. Maybe this was a trick to get him to the barbershop without complaining.

But she drove past the barbershop, too, and parked in front of the pet store.

"Here we are," she said.

Benjy looked at her. "Do you mean I can get my pet today?" he asked. He couldn't believe it. This was better than new sneakers even.

Benjy's mother nodded. "I thought you needed something to help get you through the next fifty-eight days. But remember what we talked about."

How could Benjy forget? Ever since his tadpoles had all died, his mother had been promising him a new pet. The only problem was all the things it couldn't be. It couldn't be a dog—a nice huge dog that could beat up Alex's mean dog, Duke—because a dog was too much for his mother to cope with right now, having the baby to cope with. It couldn't be a cat because cats made his father sneeze. It couldn't be a rabbit or a chick because even though they were cute when they were little, they grew up to be problems. And it couldn't be anything weird, like maybe an alligator, because weird animals made his mother sick to her stomach. It had to be small—small and quiet. Practically invisible was what his mother was after, Benjy thought.

They went inside the pet store.

"Wo-wo!" cried his sister when she saw all the animals. She pointed to the canaries, the kittens, the hamsters. "Wo-wo! Wo-wo!" It was one of only three words she knew, and she didn't get many chances to use it. She was in heaven.

Benjy felt like he was in heaven too. All these pets, and he got to choose one. He planned to take his time.

He wandered around, looking in cages. There were the hamsters, sleeping in a furry brown pile. That was one pet he would never choose. When he was in nursery school, a sweet-looking hamster named Dorothy had almost bitten his finger off. Hamsters were mean.

There were some rabbits, left over from Easter, and two straggly looking chicks. They looked like they were at the problem stage already. And a cage of baby white rats, tiny and soft-looking. A rat might be fun. He could carry it around in his pocket and feed it crumbs. Maybe he could teach it tricks. Clyde, he'd name it, after Clyde Johnson. He'd take Clyde everywhere, even to school.

He looked over at his mother. She was looking at

him, shaking her head. He should have known. His parents had both had fits when they saw a mouse in the garage. She would never let a rat in the house.

Benjy looked at the next cage. A blue-green lizard was stretched out on a log. He didn't have to ask. Too weird. But in the same cage, wound around the log like a bracelet, was a little striped snake.

A snake would be perfect. It was small and quiet. But he could do a lot of things with it. Like take it to school in his lunch box. Then when Gretchen the Pain asked to borrow his pencils, he'd say, "Sure.

They're in my lunch box." She'd probably faint on the floor, and they'd have to send for the school nurse. And on the way home on the bus, Benjy's snake would somehow escape from his lunch box and fall down the back of Alex's jacket. Yes, a snake would be a great pet.

Benjy tapped lightly on the glass. The snake didn't move, but its tongue went in and out—zip, zip.

"Hello, Clyde," said Benjy.

"No way," said his mother's voice behind him. "The house isn't big enough for both of us."

Benjy sighed. His mother just didn't know a good pet when she saw one.

"Come over here," she said, "and look at the fish."

Fish were boring compared to rats and snakes. What could you do with a fish besides watch it swim? But Benjy looked in the tanks anyway.

"How about a nice goldfish?" said his mother.

"How about a nice shark?" said Benjy.

There actually was a baby shark, in a tank all by itself. And it was only $19.95. Now, there was a terrific pet.

Benjy could see it all now. "Oh, Clyde doesn't bite," he would tell Alex. "He's a tame shark." And just to prove it Benjy would stick his hand right in the tank. Clyde would rub up against it like a kitten. "Go ahead, try it," Benjy would say, his face as serious as could be. Alex would hesitate. "What's the matter?" Benjy would ask. "You aren't chicken, are you?" Finally Alex would put his hand in. "Get him, Clyde," Benjy would order. And Clyde would have fingers for lunch.

"Now, Benjy," his mother said, "you know that's not the kind of pet I meant. A shark, of all things."

"But, Mom," said Benjy. The more he thought about it, the more perfect it seemed. "I really need a shark. Please, Mom, please."

Even Benjy's sister seemed to like Clyde. She pressed her nose against the tank. "Wo-wo," she crooned, licking the glass.

"No, Melissa. Dirty!" Benjy's mother yanked her away.

The baby started to cry.

"Look over here, Melissa. See the pretty birdies!" Benjy's mother said. Her face was smiling, but her voice was beginning to sound a little grim. "Benjy," she said over her shoulder, "when you're older, you can have fancy fish in a fancy aquarium. But right now let's start with a goldfish in a bowl. Okay?"

Benjy looked at her. He had a feeling somehow that it was a goldfish or nothing. "Well," he said. "Okay."

It was kind of a comedown, a goldfish. He had had something more interesting in mind. Still, it was a pet.

The pet-store man came with a net. "Which one will it be?" he asked.

Benjy peered into the tank. There must be a hundred goldfish in there, all different colors—plain gold, white, spotted, even black. Which one was Clyde?

"Wo-wo!" yelled Benjy's sister. She had discovered a cage of parakeets and was trying to climb up to them.

"Please hurry, Benjy," said his mother, dragging her down.

Benjy kept looking. His goldfish had to be special. Smart, full of pep, a great swimmer.

"Wo-wo!" Now the baby had her hand in the cage of a bird with a bill about a foot long.

"Benjy, please!" His mother sounded desperate.

"That one," said Benjy. He pointed to a white fish with red spots that was zipping around the tank.

The pet-store man dipped in his net and came up with Benjy's fish. He popped it into a plastic bag half full of water and popped that bag into a brown bag. "Here you are," he said, handing the bag to Benjy.

"Fine," said Benjy's mother. "Let's go home." She picked up the baby and started to pay the man.

"But, Mom," said Benjy. "What about a bowl? Can I get one of those big ones with the plants and the sand castle and the deep-sea diver on the bottom?"

Benjy's mother put down the baby.

"I'll choose the bowl," she said firmly. "You watch Melissa." She went with the pet-store man to the back of the store. "You'd better hold her hand, Benjy," she called.

"Hold my hand, Melissa," Benjy told the baby.

"Wo-wo!" laughed the baby. And she ran away.

Benjy ran after her. The baby thought it was a game. Just when he got almost close enough to grab her pink hood, she laughed and crawled under the snake cage.

"Melissa, come back here," Benjy said.

The baby laughed.

Benjy followed the sound. He thought he saw a flash of pink over by the rabbit cage, but when he got there, it was gone.

"Melissa!"

Now he didn't hear anything. Maybe she fell into the shark tank. He walked over to see.

As he did he noticed a bunch of faces looking in the front window of the store. They were smiling and pointing.

"Oh, no," said Benjy.

His sister was standing in the window talking to a large blue parrot. "Wo-wo," she was crooning happily.

"Get lost, Henry," answered the parrot in a grumpy voice.

"Come out of there, Melissa," said Benjy.

The baby paid no attention. She reached up her fat hand to pat the parrot. "Wo-wo! Wo-wo!" she crowed.

"Get lost, Henry!" squawked the parrot, jumping up and down on its perch.

"We can go home now. We've got everything," said Benjy's mother behind him. "Where's Melissa?"

"Wo-wo! Wo-wo! WO-WO!"

"Get lost, Henry!" The parrot opened its beak to take a bite out of Benjy's sister.

There was only one thing to do. Benjy tackled the baby around the knees, just like on TV, and dragged her out of the window.

The faces in the window were staring, their mouths open. One boy cheered. A lady clapped. Then they were all laughing and clapping.

The baby didn't even seem grateful to be rescued. She turned bright red and started to wail.

Benjy handed her to his mother.

His mother didn't say a word. She stuffed the baby under one arm and the fishbowl under the other, and hurried out the door.

"Wo-wo! Wo-wo!" howled the baby as if her heart was breaking.

Benjy's mother staggered to the car. She practically threw the screaming baby into the front seat, muttering to herself under her breath.

People were still standing by the window, staring. One man called out, "Nice tackle, kid!" Benjy waved to him and climbed into the backseat.

His mother sat very still in front. She looked to Benjy like someone who had just lost a war. He thought he better not say anything. She might start crying like the baby.

Benjy looked down at the brown bag in his lap. His goldfish. He'd almost forgotten. He opened it and took out the plastic bag and held it up. His fish zipped around the bag for a while, then it stopped. It seemed to be looking straight at him through the bag with its tiny round black eyes.

"Hi there, Clyde," said Benjy.

4

Benjy wore his baseball hat to school the next day.
He had a single and a pop fly and then he hit one
that was almost a home run except that Henry
caught it. Not too bad a day, not too good. But he
almost had a homer.

It rained again at second recess.

On the bus going home Benjy sat with Jason.

"Did you see that long one I kicked?" he asked.
"It would have been a homer."

"Yeah," said Jason. "Henry made a lucky catch.
Did you see my two-bagger?"

"Yeah," said Benjy. "Well, at least we beat them, three–zip."

"Yeah," said Jason.

"Want to come over and see my fish?" asked Benjy.

"I can't," said Jason. "Piano lesson."

"Oh," said Benjy. Jason had a lesson in something just about every day—pottery, gymnastics, piano. Benjy was glad his mother didn't go in for stuff like that. He planned to go home and look at Clyde.

"So long, Benjy," said Jason.

He got off. Benjy's stop was next. He started getting his things together. He really had a lot to carry today. Besides his lunch box, he had all his dinosaur books and his tyrannosaurus picture and his colored pencils and a bunch of math papers and two new library books. He'd taken out *The Big Album of Dinosaurs* and *How to Care for Your Pet Goldfish*.

Benjy struggled down the steps. It was still raining too.

"Hey, Little Man. Need some help?"

Not Alex again. Not today.

It was, though. And Brian was with him. Brian went to Alex's house a lot after school because his mother worked.

Benjy shook his head. "I'm okay," he said, and he started walking fast toward his house.

Alex walked right next to him. "You don't look okay to me," he said. "You look like a man in trouble. But I'll give you a hand." He took hold of one of the handles of Benjy's bag. "Hey, what's in here anyway? Bowling balls?"

Brian started to snicker.

Alex reached into the bag and took out a book. "*How to Care for Your Pet Goldfish*," he read. "Wow! You mean you've got a fishy-wishy of your very own? Hey, Benjy-baby. That's hot stuff."

He brought out another book. "Dinosaurs— yuck." He handed it to Brian and reached in again. "More dinosaurs. What is this, a dinosaur library?"

"We're studying them in school," said Benjy.

Alex took out Benjy's tyrannosaurus picture. He turned it around all different ways. "Looks like chicken feet," he said finally.

"It's going to be tyrannosaurus," said Benjy. "For Parents' Night."

"You have to do dinosaurs for Parents' Night?" said Alex. "That's baby stuff. Our class is doing the solar system. We get to make models of the planets and everything."

"And a life-size robot," said Brian.

"Too bad, Squirt," said Alex. "You got in the wrong class."

A picture popped into Benjy's mind all of a sudden. He would reach out and grab their two heads and bang them together so stars flew out, like they did in the cartoons on TV. Then he would run like crazy. That's what he'd do.

But something was wrong with his hands. They didn't reach out. They stayed at his sides.

"Hey, there's Duke," said Brian.

A big gray wolf was running through the yards toward them. It was really a dog. Alex's mean dog, Duke.

"Dukie-boy!" yelled Alex.

He tossed the books and the tyrannosaurus picture back in the bag as Duke jumped all over him.

Benjy took off his baseball hat. He held it behind his back, hoping Duke wouldn't notice. Duke liked to eat hats.

But Duke could sniff out a hat anywhere. He nosed around behind Benjy's back.

"No," said Benjy. He held the hat over his head.

The dog jumped up and rested his paws on Benjy's shoulders. He weighed a ton. Benjy felt like he was sinking into the ground. Worse than that, he could feel the dog's hot breath on his cheek and see his wolflike fangs an inch from his ear.

He looked at Alex. Alex was smiling. He wasn't going to help.

"Down, Duke," ordered Benjy. Only his voice came out as kind of a squeak.

Duke lunged for the hat.

Benjy dropped it into his bag, picked up the handles, and tried to make a run for it.

But he wasn't fast enough. Duke's head was all the way in the bag. He didn't find the baseball hat, but he did find Benjy's tyrannosaurus picture.

It wasn't fair. Not after all his hard work on it.

"Hey, Alex. Tell your dog to drop it," said Benjy.

"Why should I?" said Alex, grinning. "He's just playing. He won't hurt your old picture."

Duke tossed his head in the air, rattling the paper.

Then he ran into the Rosedales' yard. He looked to see if anyone was chasing him.

Benjy took a couple of steps toward him.

Duke didn't move.

Benjy took another step. He bent down. Slowly he reached out his hand.

"Drop it, Duke," he said.

Duke ran away across the Rosedales' lawn.

Benjy ran after him, lugging his bag.

Alex and Brian stood in the road, laughing.

It was just like with the baby. Duke thought it was

a terrific game. Benjy would get just about close enough to touch him. "Drop it, Duke," he would order. And Duke would take off. He was having a great time. In the meantime Benjy could see his tyrannosaurus picture getting soggier and soggier, and the teeth holes in it getting bigger and bigger.

Finally after leading Benjy through three back-yards, over a fence, and through a hedge of black-berry bushes, Duke seemed to get tired of the game. In fact he looked kind of worn-out. He was down near the duck pond across from Alex's house now, sitting still, panting. Benjy could see his sides going in and out.

Benjy walked closer. The dog didn't move.

"Nice dog," said Benjy. He figured a little flattery couldn't hurt. "Good old Dukie-boy."

The dog seemed to fall for it. He wagged his tail.

Benjy was closer than he'd been able to get before. He could see how one of Duke's fangs pierced tyrannosaurus's middle toe.

"Nice superterrific Duke," he went on, laying it on thick. Very slowly he reached out his hand. "Drop it, boy."

Just at that moment a piercing whistle came from the road.

"Here, Duke!" called Alex.

Duke dropped the tyrannosaurus picture. Right into the duck pond.

Benjy couldn't believe it. He watched it sink. Down, down into the water until it rested among the leaves at the bottom of the pond. His beautiful tyrannosaurus picture, ruined.

He looked up at the road. Alex and Brian were standing there, laughing like crazy, holding on to their sides. Duke was racing around in circles, barking.

"I'm going to get you turkeys for this," said Benjy.

5

"Zingies build better bodies eight ways," said the announcer on TV. And there was number twenty-three, Clyde Johnson, stepping up to the plate, tagging a homer into the seats like it was nothing at all, and then sitting down to a big bowl of Zingies, his muscles popping out of his shirt.

"I eat Zingies every morning," he said, looking straight at Benjy. "You should too."

A better body. That was what Benjy needed. If he had a better body—bigger and stronger—he could get home runs in kickball. If he had a better body, he could punch Alex in the nose and he'd fall right over unconscious.

Benjy shut off the TV even though it wasn't the end of the program. He went upstairs to the kitchen and got the Zingies down from the shelf.

"What are you doing?" asked his mother. She was sitting at the table, feeding the baby her disgusting orange baby food. The baby seemed to think it was disgusting too. She spit it out as fast as his mother shoveled it in.

"Just having a snack," said Benjy.

"Better make it a small one," said his mother.

Benjy poured a Clyde Johnson portion into his bowl. He got the milk and sat down at the table.

"That's a small snack?" said his mother.

"For me it is," said Benjy.

"Were you planning to have dinner with us tonight?" she asked.

"No problem," said Benjy. "I'm building a better body."

"I see," said his mother.

He did eat all of his dinner too. Plus extra helpings of chicken and mashed potatoes and rolls and applesauce. "More milk, please," he said.

His father stared at him. "Somehow this does not seem like the Benjy I used to know," he said. "Are you feeling all right?"

"Fine," said Benjy.

"He's building a better body," said his mother.

"I see," said his father.

Benjy's mother poured him another glass of milk. "Pardon me for mentioning it," she said. "But I think you've forgotten something."

Benjy looked down at his plate.

"Right there," said his mother. "That green stuff."

"Oh, that," said Benjy. "That's just my broccoli."

"It seems to me that I read somewhere that nothing builds a better body faster than broccoli," said his mother.

"Absolutely," said his father. "Goes right to the muscles."

Benjy looked at his father. He wasn't smiling. But with his father you could never be sure if he was kidding or not. Mrs. Armstrong hadn't said anything like that about broccoli when they were studying nutrition. On the other hand he didn't like to take any chances.

He ate his broccoli. And a dish of chocolate pudding with cream on top for dessert.

Benjy wasn't sure if he could get out of his chair. He felt stuffed, like every inch of his insides was filled to bursting. His body must be getting better. Bigger, anyway. He felt at least as big as Fat Matt.

He also felt like he might throw up.

"May I be excused?" he asked.

"I think it's about time," said his father.

Benjy staggered up the stairs. He went right to the bathroom. He stood next to the sink a minute to see if anything was going to happen. He hated to lose his dinner after all that work. But nothing happened. It stayed down.

Now to weigh himself. Benjy stepped on the scale. The needle jumped. It was going to hit eighty pounds at least, Benjy was sure of it.

The needle stopped at fifty-seven. Fifty-seven? That was exactly what he'd weighed the last time he went to the doctor's office.

There must be some mistake. Maybe the scale was broken. That must be it. Benjy went to his room to look in the mirror.

"Ta-*taa*!" he said, making muscles in both arms like they did in the body-building magazines that Jason's brother was always reading.

It wasn't possible. His body looked exactly the same as it always looked. No bigger. No better. His face hadn't gotten round like Fat Matt's. Nothing about him looked a single bit bigger. Except maybe his stomach, which seemed to stick out a little more. Worst of all were his muscles. They didn't pop through his shirt like Clyde Johnson's. In fact, they were totally invisible.

"How do you like that?" Benjy said to Clyde.

Clyde didn't answer, of course. He never did. He just opened and closed his mouth and wiggled his tail. But Benjy liked to talk to him anyway.

He walked over and put his face close to the bowl.

"What do you think, Clyde old buddy?" he asked him. "About building a better body, I mean."

Clyde took another turn around the bowl, nibbling at the sand on the bottom in case there was any fish food he'd missed.

"I see what you mean," said Benjy.

That was it. Probably it took time to build a better body. Time and a lot more bowls of Zingies. More broccoli, even. Old Clyde Johnson didn't get his muscles overnight.

Benjy was going to have to keep eating.

6

Benjy kept eating. Bowls of Zingies. Pocketfuls of Zingies. Zingies sprinkled on ice cream. Zingies in peanut butter and jelly sandwiches. He finished up the box in two days, and his mother had to buy more. He took extra helpings at every meal too. And he didn't let Matthew have any more of his lunches. Even the day his mother gave him cream cheese and cucumber on whole wheat. Benjy held his nose and ate it all.

After school he practiced kickball, some days with Jason and some days by himself. He practiced so much that the rubber was practically falling off his right toe, but his mother still wouldn't buy him new sneakers. And he practiced punching Alex in the nose.

He did it in the air, when nobody was looking. "Take that," he muttered to himself. "And that."

"What are you doing?" asked his mother, when one time she happened to be looking.

"Just exercising," said Benjy.

"Don't tell me," said his mother. "You're building a better body."

His body didn't seem to be getting better very fast. At the end of a week he still weighed exactly fifty-seven pounds. And he still hadn't made a home run in kickball. But he was working on it.

On Friday afternoon Jason called and invited Benjy to sleep over.

"Can I, Mom? Can I?" asked Benjy.

His mother looked doubtful. "Well," she said, "I don't know. It won't be good for your body."

"What won't be good for my body?" Benjy asked.

"All that lack of sleep," said his mother.

Benjy saw she was smiling. "I'll be right over," he told Jason.

Benjy got a shopping bag and packed up all the things he would need. His baseball cards, his teddy bear, a couple of dinosaur books, his colored pencils

and paper in case he felt like working on his tyrannosaurus picture, his fishing net in case they felt like
looking for frogs in Jason's swamp, his kickball, and
his best kicking sneakers.

Benjy lugged the bag downstairs.

"I'm ready," he said. Then he thought of something. "Can I take Clyde?" he asked.

"No," said his mother. "But you can take your
pajamas and toothbrush. Have you got them?"

Benjy went back upstairs to get them.

He stopped to say good-bye to Clyde. "Hang in
there, old buddy," he said.

"I'm ready," he said when he got downstairs.
Then he thought of something else.

He called up Jason.

"What kind of cereal have you got?" he asked.

"Bran Puffs and Wheat Doodles," said Jason.
"Why?"

"Just checking," said Benjy. "I'll be right over."

He got the box of Zingies down from the shelf
and put it in his bag.

"I'm ready," he said. "Bye, Mom."

"Bye, Benjy," said his mother, kissing the top of
his head. "Have a nice trip. And don't forget to
write."

Sometimes his mother was kind of a wise guy.

Benjy just made it to Jason's house before the bag broke.

"What did you bring all that stuff for?" asked Jason, helping Benjy pick it up off the front steps. "We don't need it." He whispered behind his hand, "I've got plans."

"What kind of plans?" asked Benjy.

"Sssh," whispered Jason. "Come to my room."

Benjy dropped all his stuff on Jason's bottom bunk.

"Listen to this idéa," said Jason. "It's really cool. We're going to make a few phone calls. First we call up Cynthia and we tell her it's Alex. And we say he really likes her and he can't understand why she never kisses him. And then we call up Gretchen and we tell her the same thing. And then we call up Alex and we say it's Cynthia and Gretchen and they both like him and they can't wait to see him on the bus Monday. It'll be so cool. He'll be scared to get on the bus. He'll probably get his mother to drive him."

Benjy had to agree it was a cool idea. As long as he didn't have to pretend to be Gretchen the Pain.

"You can be Cynthia," said Jason. "All you have to do is laugh. I'll take care of the rest." Jason liked that kind of thing. He would talk to anybody.

The only problem was getting to use the phone. First Jason's big sister was gabbing away with her friends. Then it was dinnertime. And after dinner, every time they were about ready to dial, Jason's mother came along.

She looked at them in a funny way.

"Did you want to call home, Benjy?" she asked.

"Uh—no," said Benjy.

"Come on, Benjy," said Jason. "Let's go to the basement."

"I think she's on to us," he whispered when they got downstairs. "One time I called up old Cynthia and told her that my heart burned for her. Then I gave her a few good burps. My mother heard me. Since then she's been watching me like a hawk. But don't worry. I know how to get her off our trail."

All of a sudden he said in a loud voice, "Hey, Benjy, it's eight o'clock. Want to watch *Galactic Adventure?*"

Benjy looked at him. "Sure," he said.

"Louder," hissed Jason.

"Sure!" shouted Benjy.

Jason turned on the TV good and loud. Then he motioned Benjy to follow him. He went behind the furnace, through the laundry room, and into the little room his father used for a workshop. He pointed to a telephone, sitting on the workbench. "My father had this put in so he wouldn't have to run upstairs. No one ever uses it. They've forgotten it's here."

Jason took a wadded-up piece of paper from his jeans and unfolded it.

"What's that?" asked Benjy.

"My phone book," said Jason. "Ready?"

Benjy nodded. Now that they were actually going to do it, the whole thing didn't seem so cool to him. But it was too late to change his mind.

"I'm going to call Cynthia first. Watch this."

Jason dialed the number.

"May I speak to Cynthia, please?" he said in a polite voice. He covered the phone with his hand. "This is going to be a cinch," he whispered, grinning.

"Cynthia, this is Alex."

The phone started making weird noises, like there was a chicken inside of it.

Jason stared at it. He held it away from his ear. The chicken noises got louder. Then suddenly they stopped. Slowly Jason put down the phone.

"What happened?" asked Benjy.

"She recognized my voice," said Jason. "She said if I called her one more time, she's going to call the police. And she hung up." He shook his head like he couldn't believe it.

"Oh, boy," said Benjy. "Do you think she would do that?" He could see it all now. A knock at the door and this giant policeman would be standing there, ready to slap the cuffs on Jason. And he'd be arrested, too, as an accomplice. "Maybe we better forget this plan."

Jason didn't seem to hear. He was staring glumly at the phone. "I guess I shouldn't have called her last week and told her I was the zoo keeper and a boa constrictor had escaped in her neighborhood," he said. Then his face brightened. "I'm going to call

Gretchen. She's so dumb, she's bound to fall for it."

But when he called Gretchen's house, her mother said she wasn't home. She was sleeping over at a friend's house.

"Can you tell me where I might reach her?" Jason asked in his polite voice.

He hung up, looking glum again.

"You'll never guess where Gretchen is sleeping over," he said.

"Cynthia's house?" guessed Benjy.

"You got it," said Jason.

"We really better give up this plan," said Benjy.

"No way," said Jason. "At least I want to wreck Alex Crowley's weekend."

He dialed the phone again.

"May I please speak to Alex?" he said. This time his voice was high and squeaky. Benjy didn't think even Gretchen sounded that bad.

"Hi, Alex," said Jason. "I bet you don't know who this is. . . . No, not Marcia. . . . Not Susie. . . . Not Michelle."

He covered the phone with his hand. "This guy thinks his whole class is in love with him." He snickered.

"No, not Jennifer." Jason held his nose. "Yes, I'm sure it's not Marcia. It's Gretchen. You know,

Cynthia's friend. She wants to talk to you too."

Jason covered the phone again. "He doesn't believe me. I'm going to put you on. Just say you're Cynthia."

He handed the phone to Benjy.

"Uh—this is Cynthia," said Benjy. But his voice came out wrong. It sounded like a frog. And he couldn't think of anything else to say. "Hee-hee-hee," he laughed.

And he gave the phone back to Jason.

"See?" said Jason. "Anyway, Alex, I really like you. And so does Cynthia. Oh, if only you knew how much I've been longing to kiss you."

Benjy pretended to gag. Jason was really overdoing it. He must have been watching too many movies on TV.

"No, I *said* it's not Marcia. It's Gretchen."

Jason's voice was beginning to lose its cool.

"We'll be waiting for you on the bus on Monday. Save us a seat, okay?" Jason's voice didn't sound high and squeaky anymore. It sounded like Jason. "Or else," he said, and hung up.

"Boy, what a creep!" Jason sputtered. His face was so red, he looked like he was going to explode. "He didn't believe a single thing I said. He kept on saying I was Marcia Pendergast. Can you imagine that? Marcia Pendergast!"

Benjy nodded. "That sure was a cool idea of yours," he said. "Making all these phone calls."

"Let's go watch *Galactic Adventure*," said Jason.

After *Galactic Adventure* they tried out Jason's brother's new drum set. And then they worked out with his brother's weights. "I thought your brother didn't let you touch his stuff," said Benjy, trying to lift a barbell over his head. He couldn't even get it off the floor.

"He doesn't," said Jason. "But he's away on a Boy Scout canoe trip this weekend."

After that they put on ski mittens and did some boxing with the pillows on the couch.

"Take that," grunted Benjy, giving a pillow a hard left to the jaw. "And that. And that."

"Hey," said Jason. "Not bad. Not bad at all."

"I'm practicing," said Benjy, "to give old Alex a punch in the nose."

"Really?" Jason's eyes lit up. "That's cool. When are you going to do it?"

"I don't know," said Benjy. "I've got to build a better body first."

He told Jason about all the work he'd been doing on his body and all the Zingies he'd eaten and how he kept weighing the same.

"You'll make it," said Jason. "You've got to have patience. I'll ask my brother. Maybe he'll let you use his barbells."

"I'm a little hungry," said Benjy. "Do you think your mother would mind if I had some Zingies?"

Jason's mother didn't mind. But after that she made them go to bed.

"Nine thirty," grumbled Jason, climbing into the top bunk. "It's only nine thirty. She can make us go to bed. But she can't make us go to sleep."

"Right," said Benjy. "We're staying up till midnight."

They talked and played toss the teddy bear and asked each other all the riddles they knew. The clock in the living room struck ten, and then eleven.

It got quiet in the room. They had run out of things to say.

Benjy felt his eyes starting to close.

"Just promise me one thing," said Jason.

"What?" said Benjy. He forced his eyes to open.

Jason's voice seemed to come from far away. "When you punch Alex in the nose," he said, "I want to be there."

"Sure," said Benjy. His own voice sounded far away to him.

He didn't hear the clock strike midnight.

7

At the bus stop on Monday Alex kept looking over his shoulder. It was almost as if he expected someone to jump out of the bushes and start kissing him.

"What's the matter with him?" one of the fifth-grade girls asked Benjy.

Benjy shrugged. "Who knows?" But he smiled to himself. It looked like maybe Jason's plan was working after all.

When the bus came, Alex got on first and practically ran down the aisle to the last seat.

Benjy sat down next to Jason.

"I think you ruined Alex's weekend," he said.

They both looked back. Alex was sitting with his arms folded as if he was waiting to be attacked. His eyes kept darting around, from Cynthia and Gretchen two seats in front of him, to Marcia Pendergast across the aisle. He looked kind of like a trapped rat.

"Cool," said Jason.

But he was more interested in Benjy's plan for punching Alex in the nose.

"I can't wait," he said, jabbing his fist into the seat ahead of him. "When are you going to do it? How about today?"

Benjy shook his head. "Not today," he said.

Every day that week Jason asked the same question. And every day Benjy shook his head and said, "Not today."

"What's not today?" asked Danny finally.

"You'll see," said Jason with a big grin. "Won't he, Benjy? Oh, it's going to be so cool."

Real cool, thought Benjy. He could just see himself lying on the ground, wiped out by a tap from Alex's little finger. He was starting to wish he'd never said anything to Jason about the punch in the nose.

The trouble was his body. It still wasn't ready. After almost two weeks it looked exactly the same.

And it weighed exactly the same. It was like the bathroom scale was stuck at fifty-seven pounds. And then there were his muscles. Some guys, like Clyde Johnson, had muscles like grapefruits. Some had muscles like oranges. Benjy figured his muscles were like nuts. Peanuts.

He couldn't understand it. He was on his third box of Zingies too.

On Saturday Benjy's mother asked him to go with her to the garden store.

"Do I have to?" said Benjy. He'd been planning to hang around at Jason's house and see if he could get to use his brother's weights.

"I need someone very strong to carry the bags of fertilizer to the car," said his mother.

"Well, okay," said Benjy.

He thought he saw his mother smile. Benjy wondered if she really had meant that about him being strong, or if she was just saying it so he would go with her. His mother could be sneaky sometimes.

The bags of fertilizer were heavy all right. But he carried four of them to the trunk of the car by himself, and he wasn't even tired. It looked like maybe his body was getting better.

"How was that?" he asked his mother.

"Super," said his mother. "You really are getting

strong. If you play your cards right, soon I may let you carry the trash cans down to the street."

"Oh, that's okay," said Benjy.

He couldn't wait to get home and do some more weight lifting. If he couldn't use Jason's brother's weights, he'd use the fertilizer bags.

They were almost home when Benjy saw a sign tacked on a tree. GIANT GARAGE SALE, it read. SAT. 10–4. A big red arrow pointed to the left. Benjy looked at his mother out of the corner of his eye. She was a sucker for garage sales. She would drop anything to go to one. Maybe she hadn't seen the sign.

But she had.

"Benjy," she said, "do you mind if we just stop a minute at a garage sale on the way home?"

Benjy saw that she'd already turned left. It didn't matter if he minded or not.

"I'm hungry," he said.

"We'll only stay a minute," she said. "I promise. You can wait in the car."

He had heard that before. She always said she would only stay a minute, and she always ended up staying an hour. He might as well get out of the car.

Benjy checked the pocket of his baseball jacket. Luckily he'd brought along a few Zingies in case he needed extra power at the garden store. He could use them now. He stuffed a handful in his mouth as he followed his mother up the driveway.

There were good garage sales and there were junky garage sales. Benjy had been to so many that he could tell right away which it was going to be. Good garage sales had stuff like baseball mitts and hockey sticks and piles of games and maybe an old fish tank or a broken-down guitar. Benjy had gotten a few good things at garage sales, like his baseball backstop and his world globe. The globe had different names for some of the countries because it was so old, but Benjy didn't care. The best thing he'd ever seen at a garage sale was a stuffed owl for five dollars, but his mother wouldn't buy it for him because she said it smelled. Then there were the junky garage sales. All they had were old dishes and old-fashioned clothes and rusty garden tools. Nothing for kids at all.

Benjy took one look at the old lady sitting in a folding chair next to the garage and he knew this was going to be a junky garage sale.

He was right too. Inside the garage were two card tables. On one was a bunch of kitchen stuff—juice glasses that didn't match, dented frying pans, a couple of cracked platters, some flower vases, salt-

and-pepper shakers shaped like cactuses that said
SANTA FE, NEW MEXICO on them. Stuff like that.
On the other table were piles of old books and
magazines and a box of faded-looking curtains. And
out in the grass were stacks of flowerpots, a couple
of old suitcases, a rusty lawn mower, four kitchen
chairs that looked like they would collapse if you
sat down on them, and a birdbath. That was it.

Benjy walked over to his mother, who was looking
at one of the vases. She had one exactly like it at
home, he was sure of it. "Let's go, Mom," he said
in a whisper. He didn't want to hurt the old lady's
feelings.

His mother paid no attention. "I wonder if this
would match the blue in the dining-room curtains,"
she asked herself.

Benjy checked the magazines to see if there were
any about baseball. There weren't. He went back
to his mother.

"Come on, Mom," he muttered through his teeth.

His mother was holding a pair of curtains up to
the light. She had better curtains than that up in the
attic at home. "I just know I could make something
out of these," she said. "But what?"

It was no use. There was no talking to his mother
at a garage sale. He might as well wait in the car.

He started to leave the garage. As he did he noticed something leaning up against some rakes and old tires back in a corner. It was a punching bag.

Benjy walked back to look at it. It was old and dusty like everything else. The wire that held up the bag was a little bent, and the board you stood on to hit it looked like a dog had chewed on it. But it seemed to work. He gave it a light left to the jaw, and the punching bag bounced back.

He dragged it out to the old lady.

"Is this for sale?" he asked.

She looked surprised to see it.

"Why, I'd forgotten that was back there," she said, smiling. "It belongs to my grandson, but he's more interested in motorcycles than muscles now. Yes, I think I could sell it to you."

"How much?" asked Benjy.

The old lady looked at the bag and then back at him. Probably it would be too much. He was a little short of cash right now, having just spent his last two allowances on the new issue of *Today's Musclemen*.

"What would you say to a dollar and a half?" she asked.

"It's a deal," said Benjy, before she could change her mind.

He went back to his mother.

"Mom, could you give me an advance on my allowance?" he asked.

Finally she came out of her trance. Piling one of the platters and the vase on top of the curtains, she followed him out of the garage. "I guess so, Benjy," she said. "What did you find to buy?"

"This," said Benjy.

His mother looked over the punching bag. Slowly she nodded her head. "Well," she said. "It's just what you need, isn't it? But how many allowances is it going to cost?"

"Only three," said Benjy.

"And the price is right too," said his mother. "It's a deal."

When he got home, Benjy had a bowl of Zingies. Then he set up his punching bag in the playroom. He worked out with it while the baby sat in her playpen watching him.

He pretended the bag was Alex. First he warmed up with some left jabs to his chin.

"Gloop," said the baby. She didn't seem impressed.

Benjy took off his shirt.

He tried a left to Alex's midsection and then a

hard right to his jaw. "Take that," he muttered. "And that."

"Gork," said the baby, smiling.

Benjy took off his undershirt.

He wound up, like the middleweight champ on TV, and delivered his knockout punch. "And that!"

The punching bag keeled over so, it nearly hit the floor.

"Gumbo!" cried the baby, clapping her hands.

Benjy didn't know what that meant, but he appreciated the applause. He went to the phone and called Jason.

"You've got to see this," he said. "Come on over."

"See what?" asked Jason.

"You'll see," said Benjy mysteriously.

When Jason got there, Benjy did it all again. First a few warm-up jabs. Then his left-right combination that would have Alex hanging on the ropes. And then his knockout punch.

"Take that!"

The punching bag dipped to the floor. Then it shot up again. The bag came off the wire and sailed through the air. All the way across the room and into the baby's playpen.

"Oof," said the baby, as it missed her head by a whisker and bounced off her fat stomach.

"Wow!" said Jason, shaking his head.

The baby looked at the punching bag. She didn't

seem to know whether to laugh or cry. Finally she reached out and hit it with her fat fist. "Gumbo!" she laughed.

"That was some punch," said Jason. "You nearly knocked out your sister."

Benjy smiled. It was some punch all right.

"You know what, Benjy?" said Jason.

"What?" said Benjy.

"Alex better watch out. I think you're ready."

8

"Today?" asked Jason the minute Benjy climbed on the school bus on Monday.

Benjy nodded.

"Ya-hoo!" Jason jumped up and down in his seat, as if Benjy had already delivered the knockout punch. "Today's the day!" he called to Danny down in front.

"The day for what?" Spencer and Adam turned around in their seats.

For a minute Benjy thought Jason was going to tell the whole bus. Then he said, "You'll see. Oh, boy, will you see!" And he sat down. "When are you going to do it?" he whispered loudly to Benjy. "First recess?"

"I don't know," said Benjy.

He was ready all right. Benjy could feel it. This morning when he'd weighed himself, the needle had almost hit fifty-eight pounds. And his muscles might not be that big, but they were hard. He'd spent all afternoon Sunday lifting fertilizer bags. And he'd eaten two bowls of Zingies for breakfast. He was ready all right.

The thing was, it had to be at the right moment. Benjy wasn't quite sure what the right moment was, but he'd know it when it came.

The bus pulled up in front of school. Benjy got off. Jason was right behind him, as close as his shadow. Behind him followed Danny and Spencer and Adam.

"What's Benjy going to do anyway?" Danny asked Jason.

"Flatten Alex," said Jason under his breath. He poked Benjy in the ribs. "There he is."

Benjy looked over his shoulder. Alex was getting off the bus. He was all by himself. He looked half asleep. This wasn't the right moment.

"Not now," said Benjy.

All morning it was like that. Every time Benjy

got up from his desk to sharpen a pencil, Jason was right behind him. Or Danny. Or Spencer and Adam. When he walked down the hall to music class, he practically tripped over them. Even when he raised his hand to go to the boys' room, Jason raised his hand too.

"What did you think I was doing, meeting Alex in the boys' room?" Benjy asked him.

Jason grinned. "I don't want to miss anything."

"You won't," said Benjy. "You won't."

Finally it was time for first recess. Benjy walked down to the kickball field. Of course, Jason and Danny and Spencer and Adam followed close behind. It was like they were stuck to him with glue. Benjy was beginning to feel like Clyde Johnson surrounded by his fans. He wasn't sure he liked it. Clyde Johnson's fans expected him to hit a home run every time he came up to bat.

"This is it, right, Benjy?" Jason kept asking. He bobbed and weaved, sparring with the air. Then he pretended to fall over, tagged by Benjy's knockout punch.

"Maybe," said Benjy. His stomach suddenly felt a little weird, like something was hopping around inside of it. Probably he was just hungry. He popped a few Zingies into his mouth for extra energy.

Brian was already on the kickball field, kicking the ball around with Scott and Greg from Mrs. Bloom's class. Alex wasn't there.

"Same teams as usual, right?" asked Brian.

"Right," said Jason. "Hey, where's Alex?"

Brian shrugged. "I think he's playing basketball."

Benjy looked up the hill. He thought he could make out Alex's green jacket underneath the basketball hoop.

"Basketball!" said Jason. He said it as if he'd just had a great idea. "Hey, we haven't played basketball in a long time. What do you say, Benjy? How about basketball instead of kickball today?"

All of a sudden Benjy could feel four pairs of eyes staring at him. Four pairs of eyes waiting. He knew what they were waiting for. He looked up the hill again at Alex's green jacket.

It still wasn't the right moment.

He shook his head. "Let's play kickball. Come on—Armstrongs get first ups!"

All through the game Benjy could feel the eyes on him. When he popped up his second time up, he heard Adam say to Spencer, "What do you expect? Big talk—no action." Even Jason, when they were walking out to the outfield, looked at him in a doubtful way. "You're really still going to do it, aren't you, Benjy?" he asked.

"Yeah," said Benjy. "I'm still going to do it."

At least they stopped following him around after first recess.

Then it was lunchtime.

Benjy was glad. He could use a new supply of energy. He had a feeling he was going to need it for second recess.

In his lunch box he had a peanut butter and jelly and Zingie sandwich, a container of yogurt, an apple, and a cookie. All he needed was a couple of milks to go with it. He took a tray and got into the cafeteria line with Jason.

"You're buying?" he said, looking at Jason's empty tray.

Jason nodded. "It's spaghetti."

"Gork," said Benjy, making a face like his little sister. The school spaghetti was disgusting. It was all sauce. And it smelled strangely like his sister's baby food.

"I like spaghetti," said Jason. "My mother never makes it at home."

That explained it. Benjy's mother made it at home. He knew what real spaghetti tasted like.

He watched the cafeteria lady ladling out the sauce. Matthew, who was ahead of Jason, took two platefuls. Jason took one. The fumes were overpowering.

"Let me out of here," said Benjy, holding his nose.

He felt a tap on his shoulder.

"Well, well. If it's not El Squirto. And what kind of weird sandwich did your mommy pack for you today? Bean sprout? Crunchy granola?"

Benjy didn't have to turn around. He knew it was Alex.

This could be the right moment.

He noticed that his stomach had that funny feeling again. Like an army of ants was tap-dancing inside of it. But there was no time to gulp down some more Zingies. There was no time for anything.

Very slowly Benjy turned around. In a calm, clear voice he said, "What do you care if I like weird sandwiches?"

Alex looked surprised. For a minute he didn't say anything. Then he laughed. "You'll never grow big and strong if you eat junk like that," he said. "You don't want to be skinny and weak forever, do you?"

This was the right moment. A couple of left jabs, a left-right combination, and then the kayo punch.

And in front of the entire third grade too. It would be beautiful.

Benjy looked Alex right in the eye.

"Who says I'm skinny and weak?"

Alex looked back at him.

"I do."

This was the right moment all right.

Suddenly Benjy noticed how far up he was looking to look Alex in the eye. This guy was big. Really big. And his football shirt seemed to bulge where the sleeves were rolled up. A picture flashed into Benjy's mind of muscles as big as grapefruits.

But it was too late to stop now.

"Oh, yeah?" said Benjy. This time his voice shook a little.

"Yeah," said Alex. His voice didn't shake.

There was no turning back. He couldn't run away. He was going to have to go through with it.

Benjy turned and handed his tray to Jason.

Alex handed his tray to Brian.

Benjy lifted his fists. He crouched down low, like he'd seen the middleweight champ do on TV. At least he'd be a smaller target.

"Give them room," said Jason, taking a step backward.

"Ow!" yelped Matthew. "That was my foot!"

Something flew through the air. Benjy turned around to see two plates of spaghetti, like flying saucers, sailing across the cafeteria. One landed in the middle of Marcia Pendergast's tray, splashing a big red circle on her Brownie uniform. She looked surprised. The other one bounced off the ceiling, then dripped down on Brian's shoulder.

"Hey, what's the idea?" he yelled. He picked up his plate of spaghetti and tossed it at Matthew.

"Food fight!" someone cried.

"Hooray! Food fight!"

More spaghetti, salad, and milk flew through the air.

Benjy saw Adam take a glob of red Jell-O on his

spoon, bend it back, and let it fly. Another red circle appeared on Marcia Pendergast's Brownie uniform.

"Hey, cut that out!" she cried. She put a glob of Jell-O on her spoon and bent it back.

It hit Jason right in the eye. He picked up a handful of spaghetti and tossed it at Alex. Only Matthew was in the way. Suddenly Benjy felt spaghetti sauce in his hair, dripping down his face. He couldn't see. He could only hear plates crashing and the cafeteria lady yelling and then the very loud, very angry voice of the principal.

She made everyone who had spaghetti on them go to her office. There were so many of them, they could hardly fit in the room. Brian and Alex and Benjy and Jason and Matthew and Marcia Pendergast and her friend Karen and Jennifer and Henry and Fernando and Adam. Benjy was glad to see that Gretchen the Pain had gotten some on her too. Her funny hair was full of spaghetti worms. They all had to sit and listen to Dr. Bertram talk about how terrible it was to fight and especially in the cafeteria, and how someone could have been knocked out with a plate. Then they were all sent to the nurse's office to get cleaned up and see if all the junk in their hair was spaghetti or if some of it was really blood.

In the excitement Benjy forgot all about the fight with Alex.

But not Jason. As they were walking down the hall to the nurse's office, he looked at the back of Alex's shirt and then at Benjy's.

"I'd call it a draw," he announced.

"A draw?" said Benjy.

Jason grinned. "Maybe you didn't knock out Alex," he said. "But that was the best lunch we've had all year."

9

Jason called it The Day of the Flying Spaghetti. He thought it was the coolest thing that had ever happened at school. He didn't care that they all had to eat at a special table with Dr. Bertram for the rest of the week. He said it was worth it. And he didn't ask Benjy any more about when he was going to punch Alex in the nose.

Benjy still thought about it though. What would have happened if the plates of spaghetti hadn't gone flying at that moment? He thought he knew. He would have gone flying.

How come he was so small anyway? Eating all

those Zingies and lifting all those fertilizer bags hadn't really helped. He still weighed only fifty-seven pounds, and his muscles were still as puny as they'd always been. El Squirto—that was him.

Sitting with Matthew at lunch every day didn't help. It made him feel like he was shrinking instead of growing. Finally on Wednesday he couldn't stand it anymore. He said to Matthew, "Can I ask you a question?"

"Sure," said Matthew. He was eating an ice cream cup. Benjy's mother gave him ice cream money once a week. Matthew got ice cream money every day. Some days he had two ice creams.

"How did you get to be so big anyway?" asked Benjy.

Matthew didn't stop scraping the sides of his cup with his spoon. "I don't know," he said. "I was always big."

"Even when you were a baby?"

Matthew nodded. "My mother says I was the biggest baby she ever saw. That's because I come from a big family. My father is big. My uncle is big. You know my little brother?"

Benjy had seen him. He was built like an army tank.

"How old do you think he is?" asked Matthew.

"Five?" said Benjy.

"Two and a half," said Matthew.

When Benjy got home from school, he took a good look at his little sister. She was sitting in her playpen, tossing out all her toys and laughing like crazy. She looked small. In fact, her teddy bear was bigger than she was. Even for a baby he'd have to say she wasn't very big.

"Ready for your snack?" asked his mother.

"I guess so," said Benjy.

While his mother got down the Zingies, Benjy measured her with his eyes. Not quite as tall as Mrs. Armstrong, he decided. And Mrs. Armstrong wasn't as tall as Mrs. Bloom. For a mother his mother seemed on the small side.

When his father got home, Benjy looked him over too. When he was little, he used to think his father was the biggest person in the whole world. But that was maybe because he talked loud and carried Benjy around on his shoulders. Now he saw that his father was only a little taller than his mother. For a father he really wasn't too large.

Just to make sure, at the dinner table Benjy asked, "Do we come from a big family?"

His father looked at his mother. "Big in spirit," he said, "if not in body."

"What does that mean?" asked Benjy.

"That means no," said his mother. "About average."

"I thought so," said Benjy.

"Are you ready for your seconds of meat loaf?" asked his mother.

Benjy looked down at his plate. There was a big glob of leftover ketchup on the side. It reminded him of spaghetti sauce. "No, thank you," he said. "I'm not too hungry."

"What?" said his father. "Not hungry? I thought this was the boy who was building a better body."

Benjy looked up. "I was," he said. "Only I don't think it's really working."

His father had a funny expression on his face. Like he was thinking of something far away. "I know what you mean," he said. "I wanted to be heavyweight champion of the world once myself."

Benjy stared at him. "You did?"

He couldn't believe it. His father wore suits all the time. And about the only thing he ever did with his muscles was mow the lawn. He couldn't imagine him as a boxer.

His father was smiling now. "I did," he said. "And I was pretty good too. I remember I used to practice all the time. I made a punching bag and hung it from a tree. And I used to pay my little brother five cents an hour to be my sparring partner."

Benjy couldn't imagine that either. His Uncle Dick was a dentist.

"Oh, I really had all the moves in those days," said his father.

And suddenly he got up from the table and started shadowboxing. A left to the chandelier, a right to the curtains.

"Hey," said Benjy. "Not bad."

His father danced around the table, feinting a punch at Benjy's ear as he passed. "Watch out, everyone," he said. "Here it comes—my knockout punch." He wound up and let go with a terrific right to the jaw of Benjy's mother's avocado plant.

The plant's leaves shuddered. One yellow one fell off.

"It's a knockout!" cried Benjy. "Nice one, Dad."

The baby pounded her tray.

"Oh, Jim," said Benjy's mother.

His father sat down, breathing hard.

"So what happened?" asked Benjy.

"Nothing happened," said his father. "I never got big enough to be a heavyweight. Or even a middle-weight. And somewhere along the way I decided it

was more fun using this"—he pointed to his head—"than my fists."

"Oh," said Benjy. The end of the story was kind of a letdown. He'd been hoping his father had at least knocked out someone. That would be something to tell Jason.

"Well," said his father, as if he knew what Benjy was thinking, "I did beat up Tiger Devlin when I was eight."

"Really?" said Benjy, his hopes rising.

"Really," said his father. "Of course, she was only six at the time."

"Oh," said Benjy. He decided not to tell Jason after all.

The next morning at school Mrs. Armstrong was talking about diplodocus.

"This was the biggest dinosaur ever discovered," she said. "It was eighty feet long. That's as long as four cars lined up bumper to bumper."

Benjy raised his hand.

"How come some dinosaurs were so big and some were so small?" he asked.

"Well," said Mrs. Armstrong, "each animal is born with a kind of plan built inside of it, called its genes. The genes tell if the animal will be big or small, if it will have feathers or fur or scaly skin, and everything else about it. The animal gets those genes from its mother and father. So the size of the dinosaur depended on the size of the dinosaur family."

Just as he suspected, thought Benjy. He'd been born into the wrong dinosaur family.

"By the way, Benjy," said Mrs. Armstrong. "We're waiting for your tyrannosaurus picture to complete our mural. Parents' Night is next Tuesday. When do you think it will be ready?"

"Tomorrow," said Benjy. "I'll bring it in tomorrow."

10

"You're looking good, kid," Benjy said to Clyde.

Clyde went into one of his speed runs, zipping twice around the bowl, then up for a little air, then back to take a bow.

"Very nice," said Benjy. "That's keeping the old fins in shape."

He picked up Clyde's bowl and moved him from the bookcase to the desk.

"I want you to see this," he said.

Benjy took out his art paper and his colored pencils and his dinosaur book. He sharpened all his pencils. Then he went over and closed the door of his room. He couldn't work if he could hear his mother talking on the telephone or his sister saying "Da da da" to herself a hundred times. He sat down at his desk.

Sometimes his mother came in even when the door was closed. For some reason Benjy felt like he needed to be alone. He took a red pencil and a piece of paper and made a sign. NO TRESPASSING. DON'T COME IN. THIS MEANS YOU. SORRY, it said. He hung it on the door. Now no one would bother him, for sure.

"Here goes," he told Clyde.

He started with the feet again. Dark green with purple toenails this time. He worked slowly and carefully. He had the feeling that this was going to be his best tyrannosaurus picture yet.

Finally he finished the feet. He held the paper up for Clyde. "What do you think?" he said.

The feet were perfect. Only one thing was wrong. If the rest of tyrannosaurus was as big as the feet, he wouldn't fit on the paper.

Benjy went to his closet and got another piece of paper. The biggest piece he had. It covered almost his whole desk. He might as well make a tyranno-saurus that everyone could see.

There was a light tap on the door.

"Benjy?" said his mother.

"What?" answered Benjy. At least she didn't come in.

"I just wondered what you were doing in there," she said.

"Drawing," said Benjy.

"Oh," said his mother. She sounded disappointed. Benjy thought he knew why. She was always hoping when his door was closed that he was cleaning his room to surprise her.

His mother went away, her footsteps sounding sad.

Benjy kept working. This time he got the feet finished and most of the powerful back legs before he noticed that he'd done it again. His tyrannosaurus was outgrowing the paper. There wasn't going to be room for his head.

"Oh, no," he said to Clyde.

Benjy went downstairs.

"Mom?" he said.

"What is it?" She was standing at the stove, stirring something. Pink pudding, his favorite dessert. She was making it for him even though he wasn't cleaning his room to surprise her. After he finished his picture, Benjy thought, maybe he would clean his room and surprise her.

"Can I have a piece of Dad's big paper?" His

father had special architect's paper with light-blue squares on it. It was so big, you had to roll it up.

"What for?" asked his mother.

"I'm making a tyrannosaurus picture for school, for Parents' Night."

"I guess he wouldn't mind," said his mother.

The paper was too big for the desk. Benjy had to work on the floor. His colored pencils were too light to show up on such big paper. He switched to markers.

This time he drew an outline of the whole body first. Then he colored it in. It was a lot of coloring. His green marker ran out and he had to switch to blue. It made his tyrannosaurus look kind of eerie, but Benjy decided he liked it. A two-tone dinosaur looked more dangerous than a regular one somehow.

Once his father peeked in. "I hear a major work of art is under way," he said. "How are you doing, pal?"

Benjy didn't even look up. He was on the front feet now, and they were tricky. "Fine," he said.

A little later his mother tapped on the door again. "Dinner's ready," she said. "Pink pudding for dessert."

"I'm not finished," said Benjy.

He couldn't stop now. He was about to start on

the teeth, each of which was six inches long, Mrs. Armstrong said, and sharp as a dagger.

"I'll keep your dinner warm," said his mother. "Come as soon as you can."

He picked yellow for the teeth. Very carefully he drew about twelve long yellow fangs, with points as sharp as daggers. He made the mouth smile in a nasty way. And just for good measure he added a few drops of saliva dripping off the chin so it looked

like tyrannosaurus was drooling for a tasty duck-billed dinosaur for dinner.

That gave him an idea. He went into the closet and dug around until he found the little set of paints he'd gotten for his spaceship model. It had colors that glowed in the dark. He got the jar of gold and went over the teeth with it. Now his picture would look scary even in the dark.

That gave him another idea. He went back into the closet and found his junk box. This was where he kept stuff that he didn't know what to do with but that was too good to throw away. He took out some cardboard sunglasses that he'd once gotten in a junior detective kit. They were supposed to be a disguise. The glasses had weird eyes made out of some glittery material. The eyes seemed to move as you moved, so they were always looking at you. Benjy cut out the eyes and pasted them on his picture. Now no one could escape the awful gaze of his tyrannosaurus.

Then, finally, he stood up to look at his picture. He had to get way back, it was so big. But he could see right away. It was perfect. The best tyranno-saurus picture he'd ever made.

He held up the picture for Clyde to see. Clyde seemed to have dozed off, but when Benjy tapped on the bowl, he did a backward flip and a reverse speed run.

"Terrific tail action," said Benjy.

He carefully rolled up the paper and took it down-

stairs. His mother and father were just finishing
dinner. His sister was sitting in her high chair trying
to stuff a string bean in her ear.

"Did you finish?" asked his mother.

Benjy nodded. He unrolled his picture.

"Benjy!" said his mother. "That's really super.
Your best yet, I think."

"Terrific," said his father.

"Wo-wo," said the baby. At least she recognized
it was some sort of animal.

"Wait," said Benjy. He went to the light switch and turned off the chandelier.

Twelve terrible fangs glowed in the dark.

"My goodness," said his mother. "It certainly is lifelike."

"Kind of makes me lose my appetite," said his father.

Benjy turned the light back on.

"Not me," he said. "What's for dinner? I'm starved."

11

"Hey, Baby Ben! What're you taking to school this time, your teddy bear?"

Benjy might have known. He had his tyrannosaurus picture carefully rolled up inside the biggest shopping bag his mother had, but still Alex had to say something.

"No way," Benjy started to answer.

But just then one of the fifth-grade girls yelled, "Bus! Here comes the bus!" Alex rushed to the curb, losing interest in Benjy's bag. He always had to be the first to get on.

Saved by the bus. Benjy leaned down and tied his

sneaker, which wasn't untied. He wanted to be the last one on. Going up the steps, he checked to see where Alex was sitting. He was in the last seat as usual. Jason waved to Benjy from the back, but Benjy shook his head. He took the seat right behind the driver.

When they got to school, Benjy was first off the bus. He hurried to his classroom. No one was there except Mrs. Armstrong, who was tacking up a sign over the dinosaur mural.

"Good morning, Benjy," she said.

"Good morning," said Benjy. "I brought my tyrannosaurus picture."

"Oh, good," said Mrs. Armstrong. "Just what we've been waiting for."

Benjy took all the wrappings off his picture and unrolled it.

"Oh, my," said Mrs. Armstrong in her low, quiet voice.

And that was all.

Benjy wished all of a sudden that he hadn't made his tyrannosaurus two-tone. And those shifty eyes and the glow-in-the-dark fangs. They were really a dumb move.

But now Mrs. Armstrong was saying something else. "Benjy, this was worth waiting for. You've done a wonderful job. This is quite a glorious tyrannosaurus."

"Quite glorious." It was the best thing Mrs. Armstrong ever said about anything. She liked his picture.

"The fangs glow in the dark," he said.

The rest of the class liked his picture too. Mrs. Armstrong turned out the lights so they could see the fangs glow.

"Hey, cool," said Jason.

"Weird," said Danny. That was the best thing he ever said about anything.

"I think the way you blended the blue and green is artistic," said Gretchen the Pain, who thought she was an artist. Benjy didn't tell her he'd run out of green.

The only problem was that the tyrannosaurus was too big for the mural.

"I have an idea," said Mrs. Armstrong. "Let's hang it on our door. That way we can share Benjy's tyrannosaurus with everyone."

So Benjy taped his picture on the door, along with a sign he wrote in script himself that said WELCOME TO THE MESOZOIC ERA.

Everyone from Mrs. Bloom's room next door and Mr. Duffy's room across the hall stopped to look at Benjy's tyrannosaurus. They all liked it too.

All except Alex.

"Gross, sickening," he said in a loud voice to Brian. "A seasick dinosaur."

Benjy thought how really great it would be if his tyrannosaurus opened its mouth and grabbed Alex with his terrible six-inch fangs. Alex would struggle and yell for help, but it would be no use. Nothing could save him. Gulp, crunch, swallow—good-bye, Alex.

If only his tyrannosaurus was real. If only. If only.

Benjy was still thinking about it at lunchtime. So it took him a few minutes to notice that something was wrong with Matthew. Instead of double helpings of the hot lunch, extra bags of pretzels and potato chips, and two ice creams, all he had on his tray was a sandwich and an orange.

"What happened?" Benjy asked him.

Matthew looked up. He looked terrible, kind of like Benjy's sister when you took away her teddy bear. "My mother put me on a diet," he said.

Benjy thought about that for a while. In his pocket were two dimes and a nickel that his mother had given him for ice cream. He jingled them around. Then he took them out and stacked them up on the table.

"Hey, Matt," he said. "I'll buy you an ice cream."

"Really?" Matthew looked better already.

"I'll buy you an ice cream," said Benjy, "if you punch Alex Crowley in the nose."

Matthew looked at the money and he looked at his orange and he looked at Benjy. Then his face broke into a pumpkin grin. "Okay," he said. He jumped up and headed for the ice cream line.

"Hey," said Jason. "Do you think he'll really do it?"

"Sure," said Benjy.

"When?" asked Danny.

"Second recess," said Benjy.

"Oh, boy, oh, boy!" said Jason, bouncing up and down in his chair. "This is going to be cool. It may even beat The Day of the Flying Spaghetti."

At second recess Benjy waited for Matthew to go outside. He seemed to be having trouble zipping his jacket.

"You go ahead," he told Benjy.

"That's all right," said Benjy. "I'll wait."

When they got outside, Jason and Danny and Spencer and Adam were waiting for them. And Scott and Greg and Henry and Fernando and Jennifer and Marcia Pendergast. It looked like Jason had told the whole world.

Alex was down on the kickball field, bouncing a ball around.

"Now?" asked Jason.

"Now," said Benjy.

"Does it have to be in the nose?" asked Matthew. "I can't stand blood."

Benjy nodded. He didn't know why, but for some reason he wanted it to be in the nose.

Slowly Benjy and Matthew walked down to the kickball field. Jason and Danny and Spencer and Adam and Scott and Greg and Henry and Fernando and Jennifer and Karen and Marcia Pendergast followed.

Benjy noticed that his stomach wasn't jumping around this time. He felt perfectly calm. Matthew, on the other hand, looked like he wished he were back in the ice cream line. He was walking slower and slower.

Benjy reached into his pocket.

"Zingies?" he asked.

"Thanks," said Matthew.

Then they were at the kickball field.

"Hey, Alex," called Benjy. "I've got something for you."

Alex stopped bouncing the ball.

"What?" he asked.

And Matthew gave it to him. Right on the nose. It was beautiful. Alex keeled over, just like on TV. And his nose started bleeding. It was bleeding like crazy. Probably he'd have to go to the school nurse.

"That's what, Potato Face," said Benjy.

12

Alex did have to go to the school nurse. She made him lie down in her office and he missed all of second recess. He told everyone that he fell off the slide. No one, except maybe his teacher, believed him though. Everyone else knew about Matthew's punch.

Everyone on the bus going home knew about it too. Benjy and Matthew and Jason and Danny sat in the last seat and told the story over and over. "Right in the snoot," Jason kept saying. "It was the coolest thing I ever saw. The Day of the Great Punch in the Nose."

Alex sat up front behind the driver. And all the

way home he didn't say a single word.

It was like that on Monday too. And Tuesday. Alex stayed far away. There were no names, no little surprises down the back of Benjy's jacket—nothing. It looked like the Great Punch in the Nose had done its job, at least for now. Alex was out of Benjy's life.

Tuesday night was Parents' Night. Benjy's mother sat at his desk next to Gretchen the Pain's mother, who had funny hair just like Gretchen, and looked at his math workbook. His father stood up and read the book about Jack and Sue and their dog Brownie. He didn't seem to like it any more than Benjy did. He kept sneaking looks at his watch. But finally Benjy was almost finished with Jack and Sue and Brownie. Mrs. Armstrong said next week he could start the book about Tim and his horse.

Benjy showed his mother and father the story he'd written about if he lived in the days of the dinosaurs. And the giant space station he'd made out of straws for his science project. And of course, his tyrannosaurus picture.

Everyone was talking about Benjy's tyrannosaurus. Parents who didn't even belong to Benjy's class stopped in the hall to look at it. Benjy heard them saying things like, "Oh, my, doesn't that look real!" and "I'd stay away from those teeth, Jimmy, if I were you." When Jennifer's little sister saw it, she started screaming, and no one could get her to stop. Even the principal, Dr. Bertram, stopped by to congratulate Benjy. She shook his hand as if he were another grown-up and said, "Very fine work, Benjy. Maybe you'll be an artist someday."

"I can't," said Benjy. "I'm going to be a baseball player."

"I see," said Dr. Bertram. "Well, maybe in the off-season."

"Maybe," said Benjy.

Parents' Night was good.

But the best thing happened the next day. It was first recess, and the Armstrong team was playing the Bloom team in kickball. The Armstrongs were trailing, three to one, with two outs and Danny on first base. Benjy was up.

"Come on, Benjy. Smack it!" called Danny.

Alex didn't say anything. He just pitched the ball.

Benjy let loose. It was a good hard one, between second and third base. Brian made a leap for it—but he missed. It went by him and into the outfield. It was good for a double at least.

"Run, Benjy!" yelled Jason.

Benjy ran. He got to second and saw Brian still chasing the ball in the outfield. He kept going.

He got to third. Danny had already scored. Brian was throwing the ball in to Scott, who was covering home plate.

"Keep going!" cried Jason.

Benjy slid into home plate in a cloud of dust, just like Clyde Johnson. The throw went over Scott's head.

He was safe. It was a homer.

Jason and Danny pounded Benjy on the back.

"Nice hit, Benjy!" said Jason.

"Good slide," said Danny.

Benjy couldn't believe it. His first homer. A game-tying homer. He brushed the dirt off his pants the way Clyde Johnson always did on TV. "Come on, Jason," he said. "It's tie score. Go cream one."

Jason got a triple and then Spencer hit a pop fly that Henry dropped and then the recess bell rang. The Armstrongs had won, four to three.

When Benjy got home, he had a bowl of Zingies and told his mother all about it.

"I kept running and running and then I slid into home plate and it was an inside-the-park homer," he said.

His mother looked at his jeans. "I could tell you slid into something," she said. "That sounds super. Now go change your pants so we can get going to the shoe store."

"The shoe store?" said Benjy. "What for?"

"To get the baby some shoes and you some new sneakers," she said. "You keep saying those are worn-out."

Benjy looked down at his sneakers. The rubber was all the way worn off the right toe, and the left sole was starting to come loose. But they looked great to him. He thought he might wear them for the rest of his life.

"Worn-out?" said Benjy. "These sneakers aren't worn-out. They're just starting to get good."

About the Author

Jean Van Leeuwen is the author of many books for young readers, including *The Great Rescue Operation* and *I Was a 98-Pound Duckling*. She has also written three Easy-to-Read ® books, most recently *Amanda Pig and Her Big Brother Oliver*.

Ms. Van Leeuwen was raised in Rutherford, New Jersey, and attended Syracuse University. She has worked as a children's book editor in New York City, and currently lives in Chappaqua, New York, with her husband and two children.

About the Artist

Margot Apple was born in Detroit and received her Bachelor of Fine Arts from Pratt Institute in New York City. She has worked at a variety of jobs including cook, school bus driver, and nurse's aide. She presently lives in Pittsfield, Massachusetts.

Ms. Apple has illustrated a number of children's books, including *The Great Rescue Operation* by Jean Van Leeuwen.